Groundwood Books is grateful for the opportunity to
share stories and make books on the Traditional Territory
of many Nations, including the Anishinabeg, the Wendat
and the Haudenosaunee. It is also the Treaty Lands of the
Mississaugas of the Credit. In partnership with Indigenous
writers, illustrators, editors and translators, we commit
to publishing stories that reflect the experiences of
Indigenous Peoples. For more about our work and values,
visit us at groundwoodbooks.com.

Birds on the Brain

Birds on the Brain

·

Uma Krishnaswami

Illustrations by JULIANNA SWANEY

Groundwood Books
House of Anansi Press
Toronto / Berkeley

Text copyright © 2024 by Uma Krishnaswami

All rights reserved. No part of this publication may be reproduced, stored in a retrieval system or transmitted, in any form or by any means, without the prior written consent of the publisher or a license from The Canadian Copyright Licensing Agency (Access Copyright). For an Access Copyright license, visit www.accesscopyright.ca or call toll free to 1-800-893-5777.

Published in 2024 by Groundwood Books / House of Anansi Press
groundwoodbooks.com

We gratefully acknowledge for their financial support of our publishing program the Canada Council for the Arts, the Ontario Arts Council and the Government of Canada.

 Canada Council **Conseil des Arts**
for the Arts du Canada

With the participation of the Government of Canada
Avec la participation du gouvernement du Canada | Canadä

Library and Archives Canada Cataloguing in Publication
Title: Birds on the brain / Uma Krishnaswami.
Names: Krishnaswami, Uma, author.
Identifiers: Canadiana (print) 20230519970 | Canadiana (ebook) 20230519989 | ISBN 9781773069449 (hardcover) | ISBN 9781773067391 (softcover) | ISBN 9781773069456 (EPUB)
Subjects: LCGFT: Novels.
Classification: LCC PZ7.K75 Bi 2024 | DDC j813/.54—dc23

Cover art by Julianna Swaney
Edited by Emma Sakamoto
Designed by Michael Solomon and Lucia Kim
Printed and bound in Canada

Groundwood Books is a Global Certified Accessible™ (GCA by Benetech) publisher. An ebook version of this book that meets stringent accessibility standards is available to students and readers with print disabilities.

Groundwood Books is committed to protecting our natural environment. This book is made of material from well-managed FSC®-certified forests, recycled materials and other controlled sources.

For Ananya and Rohan

1

Iridescent

"Reeni," my mother calls. "Where are you?"

I mumble something loud enough for her to hear, but just barely. I snatch my last few precious minutes before I have to reply, have to go down, have to, have to, have to. So many have-tos in the world.

But here on the rooftop, I am in a different world. A taller world, away from all the have-tos. A quieter world. Even the traffic noises on the road below are far enough from me that I can ignore them.

I adjust my binoculars. I squint through

blurry layers of green. Where is that little bird? I saw it fly here to perch a minute ago. And now it's gone — escaped from me.

Dark feathers. Too small for a mynah. Smaller than a sparrow. Short, stubby tail. Come on, come on, I beg it silently. Who are you? Show me those feathers. Are you a sunbird? Will sunlight make your black feathers shine blue? Show me a little shine!

I'm betting it *is* a sunbird. Where are you, bright feathers? Trying so hard to spot a quick shimmer makes me feel — well, a tiny bit shimmery myself. Iridescent. That's what. Are you iridescent, birdie?

My friend Yasmin, who is a champion in the word department, told me *iridescence* is a thousand-rupee word for shiny. A kind of shape-shifting shiny, blue to red to green. The kind that needs just the right light, and you have to be lucky enough to catch it from the right angle. Will I be that lucky person today?

"*Reeeeee*ni!" My mother is calling louder now. She is using the kind of grown-up voice that means business, so I have no choice. I have to reply. "Com*iiiing*, Mumm*yyyy*!"

I give up on the bird and quickly wave goodbye to my quiet terrace bird-watching spot. Bye, raintree as tall as the building. Bye, leaves like feathers that fold shut every evening and open up again only at sunrise.

Bye to the monkeys, sitting on the next rooftop and giving me looks like they're trying to see if my binocs are edible.

Bye to the lizard, napping on the wall.

I, Reeni Thomas, of 3B Horizon Apartment Flats, see all of you from my special rooftop place.

I take the stairs two at a time, down and down again to where Mummy is waiting.

"Always on the roof," she says. "Never listening to me. Sometimes when I call

Birds on the Brain

you, it's like talking to the wind."

I smile my best smile. She brushes a leaf out of my hair.

"Come on, come on," she says. "Time to do your homework. Don't forget, you have school tomorrow. That means you have to be up early."

As if I don't know that. Early is fine with me — early is the best time to see birds and squirrels and lizards. But my mind is still on the sunbird that got away.

"Iridescent," I say. "Isn't it a wonderful word?"

She shakes her head as if she cannot understand how such a tidy, organized person like her could possibly have a daughter like me, wild about all things with feathers and talons and beaks.

2

Least Concern

ON THE BUS to school, I tell Yasmin how I almost, allllllmost, spotted a sunbird. She looks up from her book — she is always reading — to listen.

I tell her about how a sunbird's feathers shine in the sunlight, changing from black to blue with hints of purple and magenta, like a shimmery silk sari in a movie. I used to be wild about movies *and* about wildlife — all wildlife — but ever since I saw a whole flock of parrots on the rooftop, all of that changed. I decided there's only enough time to be wild about one

Birds on the Brain

thing, so now it's birds-birds-birds.

Yasmin closes her book, which means she is about to ask a question. "Are they endangered? Or threatened, or anything like that?"

"No," I say. "LC."

Now she looks puzzled. It turns out — surprise, surprise! — I've said something that Yasmin doesn't understand. This does not happen often, so I am happy to explain. "LC stands for 'least concern.' That is what bird people say for a bird that is doing fine."

Purple sunbirds can be found all over India. They are not in danger of extinction. They build nests everywhere. They hang them from tree branches. Sometimes they put them inside spiderwebs.

"Inside spiderwebs, imagine!" I say. "Two eggs in a spiderweb cradle." I hold up my fingers to show how small those eggs must be, and we both scrunch up our noses at the pure magic of it.

Sunbirds hatch enough new babies to keep their numbers up. They are not threatened. That's why they are coded LC. My words come tumbling out all over these wonderful and amazing facts.

"Least concern *and* iridescent? Most excellent," says Yasmin, which makes us both giggle.

Sometimes we get this way, Yasmin and me. One of us will start and then the other one will catch the bug. Laughing is like running downstairs at top speed. It's hard to stop.

From across the aisle, our friend Anil cries, "Hiya!" He karate-punches the air, which is his way of asking *What's so funny?*

We try to explain about birds and extinction and least concern and most excellent, not to mention iridescent, but as the bus pulls up outside our school and we prepare to get off, we are laughing too hard to talk. Anil rolls his eyes at us but he is grinning too.

"Hey, watch your step, you three," our bus driver cautions. "Life is not a joke, you know. You birdies need to work hard in school!"

That sets us off all over again, so by the time we reach our classroom, Yasmin and I are still overflowing with giggles and even Anil is chuckling.

It's nice when all of us three are happy at the same time.

3

The Survey

"SIT DOWN QUICKLY, everyone," says our teacher, Mrs. Rao. "I need to talk to you about a very important class project."

I sit down quickly and so do Reeni and Anil.

Mrs. Rao wants us to pick a topic — something we care about. Then she wants us to do a survey about that topic. We have to make a list of questions. We have to put those questions to people up and down our street. We have to collect the results and report them back to the class. We have only two weeks to do all this.

Birds on the Brain

Mrs. Rao is a champion coach of brainstormers. She likes to make us think. She is happiest when we are storming away, catching ideas as fast as we can.

"What can you ask people about? Think. Think fast!" She walks up and down between the rows of desks, as alert as a birder with a new pair of binocs. She is eager to snag a good idea the minute it appears.

Pretty soon, hands begin to go up like tree branches. Ideas fly like city pigeons.

Looking very pleased, Mrs. Rao writes all our suggestions on the board. Movies, songs, games. Health. Exercise. Transport. Diet. So many things we can ask people about. We can ask them what they think about these things. We can also ask them how much they know. It seems there is an endless list of topics we can choose from.

"You can work in pairs or in groups of three or four," says Mrs. Rao.

My hand shoots up.

"Yes, Reeni, friends can work together."

How does Mrs. Rao know what I am about to ask her before I ask it? But that is good. We can be a team of three — Yasmin, Anil and me.

"Birds," I say. "I want to survey people about birds."

"Very good," says Mrs. Rao. She tells us we have to narrow down our topics. What *about* birds? What is the focus of my survey, which means, what is the point of it? What do I want to find out?

"You don't have to tell me now, Reeni," she says. "This is for you all to think about."

Mrs. Rao means to turn us all into independent thinkers. My father says that is a lofty goal.

Yasmin says she wants to survey people about books and reading. But I want to ask them about birds. We decide we can do both. Of course. When we find out

Birds on the Brain

what they think about birds and how much they know, we can give them a list of bird books.

But Anil shuffles his feet. "I want to do a survey about martial arts," he says, sitting up straight at his desk, not looking at me.

"Anil," I say, "birds don't do karate."

"Or read books," says Yasmin.

Anil turns sideways and narrows his eyes at us. "I know that," he says. He crosses his arms. He looks down at his desk.

Mrs. Rao says not to worry. "I'm sure there are other martial arts fans in our class." She says she'll find him a group.

Yasmin looks at me. I look back at her.

All at once, I don't feel like laughing.

4

Pigeon Splat

AFTER SCHOOL, it's just Yasmin and me, when really, it should have been three of us working on this project together.

"Yasmin," I say, as we get on the bus to go home, "you're going to stick with me on this bird survey, aren't you?"

"Stick with you?" she says, flapping her arms like wings. "Of course. Like a pigeon splat in your hair."

That gets me laughing. Pigeon splat in the hair is a thing that really happened to us both when we were on a school picnic. I will never forget that smell.

"Yasmin," I say, when I can talk at last. "You are not pigeon splat. You are a good friend."

"Come on, you birdies, hurry up," says the bus driver. "One, two, three, four —" He is click-click-clicking, one click on his phone for each kid passenger.

"Are you counting us?" I ask.

"What else?" he snaps. "You think I'm counting mosquitoes?"

It seems the school has given our bus driver a brand-new phone with a special app and a special job to go along with it. He has to log each of us on the bus and off the bus.

"How much do I hate this phone?" he asks.

"How much?" I ask back.

He sputters and hisses as if he has a storm inside him.

"It makes my eyes hurt," he says. "If I could, I would go to the beach and throw it into the ocean." Then he sings in his saddest voice, "If my eyes hurt, no dreams will come to me …"

We hurry up and find seats so we can get far away from his misery.

"Does he have to do that every day?" Yasmin asks. "Count us, I mean?"

"Sounds like it," I say.

"B-o-o-o-oring," we say together. Clicking us kids on and off the bus sounds every bit as boring as counting mosquitoes. But that thought of doing something every single day gives me an idea. The idea is connected to Book Uncle.

I should explain. Book Uncle used to be a teacher. Now he runs the most perfect little lending library in all of India. Yasmin is his Number One Patron, because she reads a book every day. Every single day. No maybes. I am not that fast but I'm working on it.

"Yasmin," I say, "can Book Uncle find

Birds on the Brain

us some good bird books?"

"I'm sure he can," she says. "How about three books every day, one for each —" She stops.

"Na-na-na-na-no," I remind her.

She frowns. "Sorry, habit," she says. "We're always three."

"I know," I say. A team of two feels — not quite complete. "But it's his choice, right?"

From the corner of my eye, I see that Anil is sitting in a window seat three rows ahead of us, looking out as if there is something fascinating on the street.

It is his choice. Of course it is. But how can we do this without Anil? We always do really important things together. On the other hand, it would've been impossible if he'd joined us. How can you mix karate and birds? What kind of sense would that make?

Still, I feel pigeon-splatted.

5

It's a Sign

EVERY DAY, WHEN Yasmin and I get off the bus, we turn to wave at Anil, and he karate-punches at us through the bus window. It's his way to say *Goodbye, see you tomorrow*.

But today is not every day. Anil sees us waving. He sees us. I can tell. But then he does a karate block. Not a happy punch, but a block. He crosses his arms in front of him. He turns his head and looks straight ahead.

The bus pulls away.

Was Anil frowning? Was he upset?

Upset with us? Why? When he is the one who decided not to be on our survey team?

"Never mind," Yasmin says. "Let's go see if Book Uncle wants to be on our team." I know what she means. We could use help. We have helped Book Uncle before, and he will surely help us now.

Book Uncle is right where he should be. He is behind the counter in his little kiosk with the sign that reads:

Books. Free.
Give one.
Take one.
Read-Read-Read.

A bunch of people are waiting to return books or take books or both.

Book Uncle is our ally. Of course he is. But at the moment, he is one busy ally. We decide to catch him later.

We squeeze past the crooked tree that juts out into the road. It has a sign on it,

too. The sign reads *Caution. Protruding Tree.* That is a silly sign. Surely anyone coming along in a car or on a scooter or a bicycle, or even on two feet like us, can see that is a tree. And that it's protruding, which Yasmin says means it is sticking out.

The protruding tree is often full of parrots, but today the road is super busy. Any sensible parrot would have flown up high, as far away as possible from the crowds. Between the honking of horns and the *kreech-kreech* of brakes and the voices of people, I can't hear a single parrot sound. I wonder if they can even hear each other, with so much human noise.

Right then, in the middle of all this wondering, I see something. It wasn't there this morning. I'm sure of it. It is a new ad plastered across the front of the bus shelter roof. Bus shelter ads are usually for banks or jewelers' shops, fizzy drinks or soaps. This one is for none of those things.

This one is not even selling anything.

As I take a closer look, I see a picture of a lake with a tree in the middle. The sky and the tree and the lake are all full of birds. Where is this place? The poster has one of those codes you can scan on your phone that will take you to a website — if you have a phone, which we do not. And there are a couple of dates.

Running along the top are big, beautiful letters. Here is what they say:

Bird Count India! Do Your Bit!

"If that is not a sign," I say, "then I am DD."

Yasmin looks blank, so I quickly explain. "Another birding term. Like LC is least concern. DD means 'data deficient.'"

6

Focus

WE OPEN THE gate to Horizon Apartment Flats. As we close it behind us, the istri lady spots us from her booth, where she is busy ironing clothes for her many customers up and down St. Mary's Road. She nods a quick greeting. We wave back. No time to chat — too much to do. I know exactly what that ad means, so I explain it all to Yasmin as fast as I can.

"February eighteenth to twenty-first," I say. "Those are the dates for Bird Count India. It's part of a global event — the

Great Backyard Bird Count. It happens every year in February."

"Global?" says Yasmin, impressed. "The whole world? Really? Worldwide?"

That is correct. Thousands of bird-watchers will be out all over India with cameras and binoculars and phones. They'll all be counting birds. All that data goes into a worldwide database. The beauty of it is that *worldwide* means right here, as well — everywhere! Could there be a finer thing to do than this?

I stop. Sometimes a really good idea will have that effect. It makes your feet stand still.

"Yasmin," I say. "That's our focus."

"What's our focus?" She looks around as if the focus we need is going to float down from the top of the coconut tree or jump out from behind the istri lady's booth.

I tell her. We'll ask people what they

know about Bird Count Day. Then we'll sign them up to be part of it.

"The actual count — we can be part of it, too, Yasmin," I say. "I'm sure we can get someone to help us log our numbers on the app. But we have to hurry. The eighteenth is only a few weeks away. Okay?"

She considers this. Then she wrinkles up her nose at me and says, "Okay. That's fine. But books are still going to be part of it, right?"

She walks away. I hurry after her.

"You chickens have a minute?" the istri lady calls after us. "I have a question for you."

"We'll come back," I promise. "Later. Honest."

I run after Yasmin. "Books?" I say. "Of course, books. I said so, didn't I?"

"As long as there are books ..." she says, giving me a sideways look.

"What do you mean?"

"Nothing, just saying," she says.

I heard her. I knew she was just saying. But what did she mean?

7

Questions, Questions

AFTER DINNER, DADDY slices up sapota, which is my very favorite fruit. Its soft brown sweetness makes my mouth happy.

"Mummy," I say, swallowing the last delicious scrap. "Do you still have the old mobile phone? You know, from before you got the new Spark TV phone?" My mother works for one of our local TV stations. They keep her up-to-date with all things tech.

"Yes, why?"

"Can Yasmin and I use it for our survey? We need a phone to download a bird app."

My parents look puzzled, so I tell them about Bird Count India. I tell them how we'll make up our survey questions. We will talk to people up and down St. Mary's Road. Mrs. Rao will teach us how to tally the results. But we need a phone so we can add our very own bird counts to the worldwide database.

They listen. At first, Daddy says, "That is very impressive," and Mummy says, "Yes, yes, very." But the more I talk, the more I start to see them looking at each other the way that grown-ups do when they think you are delightful, but they are not really taking you seriously. Have I said too much about how big this project is, how global, how worldwide?

Because now my mother says, "That's a big job. Are you sure you'll be able to do all this, just you and Yasmin? Why bring in the worldwide bird count and all?"

"It's good that Reeni is interested in a

good cause," Daddy points out. He hates arguments.

"I say keep it more manageable," Mummy insists.

I protest, "But it's happening right now, so we have to make it our focus!" I try to explain what a wonderful coincidence this is, but they still look worried.

"What about your friend Anil?" my mother asks. "How come he's not doing this with you? You three always do everything together."

Daddy leans his elbows on the table and props his chin in his hands. He gets a dreamy look on his face.

"As I always say, my Reeni, to every problem there is a possible solution lurking somewhere." He stares into the face of the clock on the wall over the dining table, as if the palm trees and boat engraved on its frame will float a solution down to us.

I try to explain that Anil does not want to join us. He wants to do a survey about karate.

Mummy says, "I think that's a great idea. Why don't you join him in that?"

Daddy looks into the fruit bowl as if he's searching for solutions. "Why not sleep on it?" he says at last.

"No, no, Arvind. I think she should keep the bird count separate." Mummy is often convinced she is right, regardless of what anyone else thinks. "Reeni, you can always do the bird count for fun. No point mixing apples and oranges."

Wait. Why are we talking about apples and oranges? I was talking about mynahs and sunbirds, swallows and swifts. But I let it go.

Are there other ways to get the app? Should I ask Lina Aunty, Mummy's younger sister? She's usually on my side.

Should we ask Book Uncle to talk to

my parents? Or is he also a fan of apples and oranges?

Questions, questions, questions, and not an answer in sight.

It's only much later, when I am tossing and turning in my bed trying to fall asleep, that I remember the istri lady and her question. I promised her we'd go back and talk to her, and we never did. How could I have forgotten?

Tomorrow, I tell myself. Tomorrow we will talk to the istri lady. She will ask us her question. I don't know if we'll have any answers, but we can listen.

Speaking for myself (because who else can I speak for?), I have so many questions of my own. What's one more?

8

Illegal

MORNING COMES, and the istri lady and her question are still on my mind. Good thing today is Saturday, so no school.

I hurry and get ready. I rush through breakfast. I cross the hallway between our apartments and go knock on Yasmin's door.

"Yasmin's gone downstairs," says Nadira Aunty, Yasmin's mother. "She said she needed to talk to Ponni about something." Ponni is the istri lady's name, but only the grown-ups use it. We would never dare.

Birds on the Brain

How come Yasmin went on her own without me?

"So how are things in the bird-watching world?" asks Nadira Aunty.

"Fine," I say, and escape before she wants any details.

Downstairs, with traffic only just starting up. Parrots screech in the raintree. As I hurry toward the istri lady's stall, I catch the scent of jasmine flowers.

I'm about to smile my friendliest smile when I notice something. The iron is just sitting there. So are the clothes.

The istri lady should be ready for her workday, which is every day, as she only takes a few holidays off each year. Her iron should be heated, loaded up with coal for its daily attack on piles of washed, starched clothes from all the apartment buildings up and down St. Mary's Road.

The istri lady is standing outside her booth. Yasmin is standing there with her.

They are looking as if the sky just fell on both of them.

"I heard about this yesterday, that's why

I thought I'll tell you to ask your parents. Maybe they know more about this terrible thing. Only now, it has really come to hit me on the head."

"What?" I don't understand.

"A new state law," the istri lady says. "It's called Clean Cities."

"Clean Cities?" I say. "That doesn't sound like a bad thing."

"That's the problem," she says. "Everyone says *Aha! That law is good*. But what about people like me? Vendors who iron clothes for other people? What about us? Because of that law, we are now illegal."

Illegal? It's a terrifying word. "Why?" I still don't get it.

"What do I put in my iron?" she demands.

Oh. Now I get it. "Coal," I whisper.

"Coal," Yasmin mouths silently.

It's true. Every morning, the istri lady and her son use little bits of sticks and paper to start a fire right in the belly of her big metal iron. They blow on it until it's sparking, and then they drop in pieces of coal from a little sack they store in the booth. They fan that fire until the coals turn bright orange. You can see them glow through the little metal grill running around the edge of the iron. All day long, the istri lady keeps stoking her iron with that coal to keep it hot so she can smooth out all the wrinkles in her customers' saris and blouses. That hot iron flattens fine creases in pant legs and shirtsleeves.

The istri lady coughs, like she often does. Could it be the coal dust? How come I've never thought of that before?

"See this pink paper?" The istri lady points to a notice taped to the side of her booth. "It's telling me that my coal iron is now illegal. Illegal! They want me — oh yes, me! — to get an electric iron."

"Can't you get one?" I blurt out, before I

can stop myself. I know at once that I have said the wrong thing. Book Uncle got one of those pink papers once. They are bad news.

"And where will I find the money?" she demands. "And what about the electrical connection? You think I can plug a shiny new electric iron into that coconut tree? You tell me that."

I start to jabber in the way that I sometimes do, just to make a sinking feeling inside me go away. Yasmin frowns at me, but I can't stop. I say small, useless things like, "that isn't fair" and "maybe something will come up" and "someone must be able to help."

But it's like looking for iridescence when you know, deep down, that there is no light at all to shine on anybody's feathers.

I do not know what it is like to be the istri lady, needing to make money to feed her family. And now she's found out, with no warning at all, that the way she does her job, the way she's done it for years, is suddenly illegal. What can she do? That is one burning question for which I see no answer.

9

The Right Book

ONE MONTH. THAT'S HOW much time the istri lady has to replace her dirty coal iron with a cleaner, greener electric one. Meanwhile, the piles of clothes are waiting, and we are not much help. She gets the fire started in her iron. We leave her to her steaming.

We turn to go back inside, but something is nagging at me. I want Yasmin to know that I am her friend. That I care about things she cares about. That when she is unhappy, I am, too. I'm not sure I have the words for all that. So I say,

"Yasmin, let's go see Book Uncle. Let's see if he has any good bird books."

She stops. She looks me in the eye. Then she grins. "Race you!"

And she's off running, and I am off after her, so by the time we get to Book Uncle's corner lending library, we are both out of breath.

"Welcome, welcome!" Book Uncle peers at us from the window of his kiosk. "What can I do for you this morning, my most loyal patrons?"

"We'd like some books about birds," we say together.

"But not stories," I add.

"Ah. Nonfiction, then?"

"Books that a bird-watcher can use," Yasmin says.

"We're doing a survey about Bird Count India," I explain.

He rummages among his piles. He pulls out two books, one for each of us.

He disappears. Just when I think he's forgotten we are standing there, he pops up again in the window with a third book in his hand. "For your friend Anil."

What can I say? Our friend Anil isn't speaking to us? Something's wrong, and I don't know what it is?

Then I see the cover. This is not a bird book.

"This is about solar power," I say. "For Anil? Really? Why?"

Book Uncle raises an eyebrow.

"What is my motto, hmm?" he asks. "Have you forgotten?"

"Right book for the right person," I say.

"On the right day," Yasmin adds.

"Precisely," says Book Uncle. "That one is for Anil. Now run along, you book-birders. Good luck with your survey."

Book-birders? We grin. Book Uncle has that effect. We thank him and head back home.

Should we have mentioned the istri lady and her problem? I know Book Uncle believes there is a book for everything and everyone, but I don't see how a book could possibly solve this particular red-hot problem.

Yasmin says she's sorry, but she can't come with me to give Anil his book. Not today. She has to go shopping with her mother, who insists that she, Yasmin, has outgrown her school shoes, even though Yasmin finds them comfier with toes sticking out through a hole or two.

"Shall we give it to him later?" she says. "Maybe in school?"

That would be easier. But then I think, I can do this. How hard can it be? Anil lives three streets away, close enough for me to walk over. I'll give him the book. He will thank me. That's all. I will say hi and bye, in a friendly way. And I will walk away. If he wants to tell me what's

Birds on the Brain

bugging him, he can. If not, that's okay, too.

But ... but ... but ... somewhere inside, curiosity is chipping at my see-if-I-care. Why solar power? Why Anil? Sometimes Book Uncle's picks make no sense at all.

10

A Whole New Possible Problem

SURPRISE! WHEN I GET home, someone is waiting for me with a big hug.

It's Lina Aunty. "I've been having a nice chat with my very own Shoba Chechi," she says. This makes my mother smile. She likes to be named and claimed as Lina Aunty's own big sister.

"I saw you outside," says Lina Aunty. "You and your friend Yasmin. Waved to you, but did you wave back? Nah — you were too busy to notice." Lina Aunty often talks in small floods.

She and my mother already know about

the istri lady's problems. They are sympathetic but what can anyone do?

"So what do you have there, Reenima?" Lina Aunty points to the books I am holding — the one that Book Uncle picked for me. It's about a very famous birder. Some people call Salim Ali the "Birdman of India." This book is written by his niece Zai, which is why it's titled *Salim Mamoo and Me*. I can't wait to read it.

Lina Aunty says, "Is that not a perfect book for you, bird girl? Truly, that Book Uncle of yours is a magician. A mind reader, that's what." Oh, Lina Aunty is my very favorite grown-up. She distracts Mummy wonderfully well. Otherwise, my mother would be worrying about how much homework I still have left to do and whether I have managed to rip my sleeve again.

Lina Aunty looks at the other book I am holding. "Solar power?" she says, surprised. "Are you diversifying or something? I thought you dumped movie mania to chase hawks and sparrows."

"It's for Anil," I explain. "I'm going to take it over."

"He lives in Serene Towers, no? I'll walk with you," Lina Aunty says. "I have to get coffee powder from Akshaya. Can't go to work on Monday without my morning coffee, you know. Can you walk back on your own?"

"Sure," I say. "Okay, Mummy?"

"No problem there," Mummy agrees. She tosses cautions after me. "Careful when you cross the road ... watch out for speeding cars."

So off we go, walking fast. We are both fast walkers.

I tell Lina Aunty about Bird Count India and our survey and how I'm trying to mash them together. Passing the Palm Tree Hotel and the petrol bunk, I explain that it's just Yasmin and me, because Anil has other ideas.

Passing the dentist's office and the medical lab and the La-la-la Restaurant, I tell her we need a phone.

We have arrived at the gate of Anil's block — Block III, Serene Towers. "It's for the app," I say. "So we can log bird sightings." My heart thumps, and it's not just from our quick walk.

I expect Lina Aunty to say, *Sure, you can use my phone.* Or even, *Hey, I'll talk to Shoba Chechi. She can lend you her old phone. No problem.*

What she says is not what I expect. Not at all. Not even a tiny little bit.

"Oh, the bird count," she says. She chews her lip. She looks thoughtful.

She squeaks the gate open. We go inside.

"What about it?" I ask. "What about the bird count?"

She shakes her head. "Last year's count. Some problem with the city. Can't remember exactly. Ask your mother. I'm sure the TV station ran the story." She shrugs. "Probably nothing to worry about. Okay, cutie-ma, I'll see you later."

She plants a smacking great kiss on my cheek and dances off in search of coffee.

My heart thumps turn into a pain in my stomach.

Lina Aunty is usually sunshine and sparkles. Today, though, she's dumped a shadow over me. The shadow of a whole new possible problem. As if we didn't have enough already.

I trudge up the stairs to Anil's flat. I ring the doorbell. I hear footsteps on the inside.

11

Local and Global

ANIL OPENS THE door and greets me with a half-hearted karate stance.

I hand him the book. "From Book Uncle," I tell him.

To my surprise, his face lights up. "Solar power, yay!" He flings both hands in the air and shouts, "Hiya!"

"Sorry, Reeni," he says, recovering. "Didn't mean to startle you."

"You didn't," I say. It's true. I'm not startled. I can see that the book has brought Anil back to his normal karate self. What I *am* is puzzled. "What's so exciting about that book?"

"It's perfect! My karate club's doing a special demo. We're going to raise money for a solar tech project."

"Really?" This is news to me.

"Yes, yes. To teach solar technicians how to install panels. In faraway villages." He stops. "You really want to know?"

"I do," I say, and my mixed-up feeling grows. I'm happy Anil is telling me all this amazing stuff. I am also wondering how come he didn't tell Yasmin and me before.

He carries on. The solar techs will then teach people in the villages how to look after the panels, how to make sure they are working properly.

"It's win-win-win," Anil explains. "Jobs for solar techs. Clean, green electricity for the villages."

"One more blow against global heating," I point out.

I'm glad that Anil is excited about this

book. I'm glad to be his book courier.

He says maybe he can persuade the Serene Towers Association to install solar panels on the roof of the building. He's going to tell the solar tech people about this, and maybe they can do the job.

"Right here?"

"Right here." Anil nods his head so hard that I worry it may be in danger of falling off.

"It was hard work, Reeni, talking my survey team into this. At first they just wanted to survey people about karate, but this way, focusing on the demo, we can ask questions about both. Karate and solar energy, right? Because you wouldn't think those two things could overlap, but — hiya! — they do!"

My own head is spinning. Maybe Anil didn't tell Yasmin and me because we weren't listening. We didn't give him a chance. Plus, I didn't exactly listen to

Yasmin, did I? Now I remember the expression on her face when I was all excited about our focus. I was so in love with my own ideas that I never gave a thought to anyone else's. I can't say any of this. I don't know how.

When I get back home, I begin to read the book about Salim Ali, and nothing is as it seems. It's not about him at all, but about his niece, who wrote the book. She was a misfit in a family of birders, so why is this such a perfect book for me? I wish I was lucky enough to have a family of birders. I'm starting to feel as if I've been pigeon-splatted. Again!

12

Taking It Personally

ON THE WAY to Sunday church, I tell my parents what Lina Aunty said about a problem with last year's bird count.

"So what was the problem?" I ask.

Mummy makes small dissatisfied noises. She says, "Bird count numbers. That was the problem."

"How?" I ask.

"There were many more participants — that was all fine and good. But bird numbers? They were down from previous years."

We're stuck in traffic now, and someone

is honking at us to move faster, only there is nowhere to go.

"Down?" I say. "Oh, no! Why?"

She shrugs. "Too much construction. Too many trees cut down. Not enough places to nest."

"That's terrible!" I cry.

"The mayor took it personally," Mummy says. "It made the city look bad."

"Wait," I say. "Didn't he want to make things better?" Isn't that what a sensible person would want to do? You see something wrong — you think about how to fix it.

Na-na-na-na-no! That is not how our mayor thinks.

Our city's mayor is Karate Samuel. (Is that his real name? Who knows? That's what everyone calls him.) He is also a movie star, although since he became mayor, he has not had much time to act in films.

Birds on the Brain

What do I think? I will admit, I am a fan, movie-wise. City-government-wise, it depends. We learned a lot during the last election season, Yasmin and Anil and me — about the promises that candidates make and how quickly they can forget those promises.

I know, too, that when elections are on his mind, which they often are, Mayor Karate Samuel will take everything personally.

The traffic begins to move again.

"I've been trying to get this on the news," Mummy says, "with your bird count coming up."

The glaring sunlight makes me sneeze. "This year's count?" I say, when I've recovered. "On the news? Can you?"

"It isn't easy," she says. "Santosh knocked the segment off the schedule twice already." Santosh is her boss at the TV station. "Maybe the city government is putting pressure on him."

Pressure? That sounds bad.

"Why?" I ask.

We pull up to the church, all shiny white with curly decorations along the edges of its sky-high front. Sloping wooden eaves cover the veranda like the brim of a hat.

"Well," says my mother, "the mayor decided it was the birders' fault for making this data public."

"What?" I protest. "If we stop talking about these bird problems, he thinks they'll go away?" I can't believe what I'm hearing.

"Something like that," Mummy says.

As we walk up the wide, flat front steps under the church's hat-brim veranda roof, we can hear the whir of pigeon wings overhead. They're nesting up in the wooden beams. The building hums with their cooing.

"You never told me all this," I say.

"You're only asking me now," Mummy protests. "I'm telling you, aren't I?"

The service passes in a blur. By the time I have inhaled clouds of incense and said the responses and swallowed the Holy Qurbana wafer and wine, I am sick with panic.

Can the city shut down the bird count? They are always shutting things down. Traffic on streets they say they are fixing, only the potholes keep getting bigger. Electricity and water when there are shortages, even if the big houses of politicians never go dark. Businesses that have no permits. They even tried to shut down Book Uncle's lending library. I'm happy to say that did not work.

On the way home, I ask, "Can they really shut down the bird count?"

"Not totally. It's not an event in a single place," my mother explains. "It's just lots of people going out over two or three days and sending data from their observations. But they can make it harder."

"Like not letting you put it on TV? Can't you do it anyway?"

"Shoba?" Daddy asks. "Any chance? Maybe not a feature, but …?"

"Can't push it," she says. "I've tried already."

"It's not fair," I say. "How can the city stop the TV station from running this story?"

"It's wrong, I agree," says my mother. "But I tried, Reeni-ma. There's not much more I can do." She looks worried.

"Are you in trouble?" I ask. "For trying to run the story?"

"I don't want to be," is all she says.

I am fed up with unfairness. It burns me up inside.

13

This Is Urgent

"IS THAT THE Yasmin and Reeni survey?" Mummy asks. "Or is it Reeni and Yasmin?"

"Either is fine," I say.

"Both is better," says Yasmin.

My mother smiles and leaves us to it.

After much discussing and scribbling and scratching out, this is what we come up with for the Yasmin and Reeni, Reeni and Yasmin survey.

Item 1: Are you a reader? Yes/No/Maybe

Item 2: Do you like birds? Yes/No/Maybe

Item 3: Have you heard of Bird Count India? Yes/No

Item 4: Would you like more information on Bird Count India? Yes/No/Maybe

Item 5: Will you join Bird Count India and help us find out as much as we can about the bird population in the city? Yes/No/Maybe

Item 6: If we give you a list of books about birds, will you read them? Yes/No/Maybe

Item 7: Do you think our city should protect bird nesting sites? Yes/No/Maybe

"It's not bad," I say.

Yasmin says it's better than that. It's pretty good, she says, but she has a question about one word. "How can you *maybe* like birds?" she asks. "How can you *maybe* be a reader? Those are yes or no questions, right?"

"No," I say. "If we want to leave a window open for someone to become a reader or join in the bird count, then we have to leave those maybes. A maybe is like an invitation, see? And this is not just about the survey. This is urgent. We need everyone to join in."

"Hmm." She does not seem convinced.

"Yasmin," I say. "One out of every eight species of bird on earth is threatened with extinction." I know this for a fact. I saw it in a TV documentary last month. The number was so awful that it stuck in my mind. "That's how urgent this is. Now do you see?"

She hesitates, then she nods. She sees. And I see something, too. Sometimes you just have to slow down and give people reasons to see.

Seeing and re-seeing our questions, we decide to pilot our survey, which means we are trying it out to see how it works.

We have four ready-made volunteers, so we print out four copies. Yasmin runs across the hall to 3A and returns with her parents. I get my parents from the kitchen, where they have just changed a lightbulb and are looking pleased with themselves.

We administer the survey, which is what you call it when you give it to people and ask them to please reply to your questions, assuring them it will not take too long.

Our parents are not the best-behaved survey-takers. They keep stopping to tell us how proud they are of us and to ask questions, like when this assignment is due. They want to know how come there's no national competition for young surveyors. They ask if we plan to present our data in tables or graphs or pie charts.

We do not have time for all these questions. Who says kids are the ones who need to learn to focus?

We bring them back on track, and when we're done, we have results to look at. We have a pilot that we can take to school, and Mrs. Rao will tell us what to do next. On the one hand, we still have a lot of maybes we don't know about. On the other hand, open up a maybe and we might find ourselves hatching some answers.

That night during the TV news, a small announcement about the bird count runs on the bottom of the screen. That's good, isn't it?

Trying to hatch answers for myself, I pick up *Salim Mamoo and Me* again. It turns out he was a superstar not just in the birding world but all the time. He knew big-big people like kings and queens and prime ministers, and he went to London and Germany and all those kinds of places far away from India.

As I toss and turn in my bed, trying to fall asleep, I think it would be useful to know big-big people. They could help us get this survey off the ground …

Or solve the istri lady's electric iron problem ...

Or convince the mayor that the bird count is a good ... thing ... for ...

14

In a Flap

NEXT THING I KNOW, it's Monday morning.

Nadira Aunty is taking Yasmin to school because she has a meeting nearby and decided she'd drop Yasmin off. Yasmin tried to argue that she could take the bus anyway, but Nadira Aunty vetoed the idea, which is what parents do, sometimes for no good reason.

On the bus, I slide into a seat next to Anil and explain why Yasmin isn't there. I expect that Anil will pull his usual karate stance, meaning *Hi* and *Good morning* and

Okay, I get it, but he does not. On Saturday, I was sure his bad mood was over. Now I'm feeling unsettled again.

Then I see his face. His mouth is turning down at the corners. In fact, he looks as if he has been whacked in the face by very bad news.

"What's wrong?" I ask.

"You know the spot on the roof I told you about?" he says. "Where I wanted to work with the solar tech group to put a solar array? Guess what?"

"What?"

"There's a bird there!"

Some people have all the luck.

"And not just that, Reeni. It's building a nest. Right there on the roof."

"What kind of bird?" I say, excited. "Anil, that's great. Can I come see it?

"No! I mean, yes, you can come see it, but it's not great. How is it great? It should be nesting in a forest or a field or some place that birds are supposed to nest. Reeni, it's not an ordinary bird. It's not a pigeon or a crow or even a parrot. You should see it. It's this little." He holds his fingers together to show me an impossibly tiny size. "It cheeped at me. Reeni, what should I do?" That is more talking than I have ever heard from Anil in a single breath.

I say, "Anil, you mustn't do anything. You have to leave that nesting bird alone. There may be two of them, see? And that nest is their home. How would you feel if it was *your* home and someone came along to bother you right when you were in the middle of building it?"

"You don't understand!" Anil wails. "That's what I mean! That's my whole point!"

"What's your whole point?" I try to be patient.

"We can't just leave it alone, that's what.

At first I thought, oh no! Now what? Then I thought, fine, it's all going to take time, right? Everything takes time. But now the solar tech training group is really excited, and what's more, the building association is on board."

None of this sounds like a problem to me. But Anil says there is a deadline. The association applied for a grant a while ago, and that money has to be used up fast. "They have to get started soon. And that bird is in the way. Can't you just — I don't know — shoo it away or something?"

"Shoo it away?" I cry.

"Reeni, it's one bird's nest against sustainable power for a whole building full of people."

I am stuck on one word. "Anil, *shoo* it away? How can you even think that?"

He wriggles. "Can't you — I don't know — shoo it gently or something? It can find some other place."

The bird and her nest come first. How is Anil not with me on this? I breathe as deeply as I need to. I reach for calm and firm at the same time. "Anil, you can't let them start doing anything until that bird is done nesting."

"Reeni, can't you see?" he yells. "I feel terrible! I don't know what to do!"

That silences me. I have to get past my own feelings and think about Anil.

"Anil," I say. "I know the solar stuff is

important to you, but that nest is important to the bird. Can you imagine people all over that roof with their equipment, hammering and thumping? And what if there's no other place for her to nest? That means no eggs, no baby birds …" Now I can hardly continue.

He nods slowly. "She does get upset," he says. "She cheeps and chatters at me and flaps her wings, and she makes these little darting movements and it takes her forever to get back to building her nest. I really want those solar panels and now I feel guilty."

That is a terrible choice. Solar panels? Birds? The world needs both. And why should Anil have to make a choice like that?

I make myself refocus. "Anil," I say in my best calm voice. "Maybe you can talk to the association. I bet they have a long list of projects. Can't they put you last? Maybe they'll do that if you ask nicely.

Maybe you should tell them about the bird. How about if they can delay just a little bit — a month? Won't hurt to ask. Really, Anil, they'll take a couple of weeks to hatch and I think only a couple more to fly away. Bird families don't hang around like people. Maybe they'll be all done in a month — that's not that long." I am really grabbing hold of those maybes now. One by one, they are making me feel better. I do not think I have ever had to be soft and soothing for so long. I'm out of breath from the effort.

But it's not working. Anil is not being soothed. He is making small choking noises. "They have to renovate the rooftop terrace before the solar team gets to work," he finally splutters when he gets his voice back. "That's supposed to start next week! My father says it's all been arranged. I don't know what to do!"

He flaps his arms at me. He is too distressed even to make a single karate move. And I can see why. I have no maybes left now. *Renovate* means rework and rebuild. And in order to rework and rebuild, you have to break up what is there already. I know because we had our kitchen renovated when I was six, and I still remember the noise and dust.

Reworking and rebuilding a rooftop where a bird is planning her nest? That gives us every reason to be in a flap.

15

Facts and Opinions

AS FLAPPY AS Anil's news is, it is also a tiny bit exciting. That is to say, I am excited. I can't help it. How often does a bird show up to nest on your very own apartment building rooftop? Well, not my very own, but my friend's, which is close enough.

I am tapping my hand on my desk, which helps me think through the layers of problems that now need solving, when I hear Mrs. Rao's voice. She is calling my name.

"Reeni," says Mrs. Rao, "if you were

paying attention, you would see that it's your turn now."

Oh. It is? Oops. Yasmin is already standing in front of the class. The survey! We have to talk about it. I scramble to take my place next to Yasmin at the board.

Mrs. Rao is very pleased that we have run a pilot. She wants us to share our results with the class.

We write out our questions on the board. We have already counted up how many people said what, so we write those numbers out as well. Then we take turns reading the results out to the class.

"All of our parents are readers. Hurray!" Yasmin says.

"Only two of them said they liked birds," I add. "One was a maybe. One was a no. I mean, really? A no?"

"Reeni, just share," Mrs. Rao says. "Just the data, please. No comments. A surveyor must remain objective."

Birds on the Brain

"Only one hadn't heard of Bird Count India," Yasmin goes on.

I don't say anything because it's not my turn, and I am trying to remain objective. But who of our parents wouldn't know? Shocking.

"Two said they wanted more information. Two said maybe," I say. I swallow my comments. Only maybe?

"But three said they'll join the bird count," Yasmin says. "One said maybe."

Maybe? Really? Come on. This is a tough one to swallow. Now I'm feeling flappy all over again.

"I am relieved that all four of our pilot survey-takers said they would read bird books," I go on. "One wrote in the margin, which she was not supposed to do: 'If I have time.'" (Na-na-na-na-no! I decide that I'll have to speak to Mummy about that. If that was the case, why not just check maybe?)

"All four said they thought the city should protect bird-nesting sites," Yasmin concludes. (What a relief! More comment-swallowing from me.)

"Thank you, Reeni and Yasmin," says Mrs. Rao when we finish. "I'm proud of you."

She reminds us that although we knew who was in our pilot, replies in the real survey will be anonymous. "Data," she says. "Facts. That's what matters."

Facts, she says, are not opinions. Anyone can have an opinion, and sometimes they are just wrong because they are not supported by facts. Our survey takes people's opinions, but then we, the surveyors, also plan to offer them facts. Books and information about the bird count!

"That is very clever," Mrs. Rao says. "It is their choice, of course, but you have thought about how you will collect your data and how you will be using it." She makes a small speech about opportunity, new and wonderful activity, and community. Mrs. Rao is very fond of any and all activities that build community.

"In the interest of community and sharing," she says, "would you like to tell the class more about how to identify birds?"

Would I like …? I would, I absolutely would!

From all my days on the rooftop, all the websites Daddy has pulled up for me, and all the books I've borrowed from Book Uncle, I know these facts like lines on my palm. I tell everyone about size and profile and flight patterns. While I do, I think that maybe what I want to do my whole life is study birds like Salim Mamoo. The thought sends a shiver through me. Maybe our survey has wings. It is flying me to new and wonderful possibilities.

Finally, I tell them how climate change and pollution are affecting birds. "Birds are like messengers," I conclude. "They tell us about the health of a place. Where birds are disappearing, those places are in trouble."

No one makes jokes. No one rolls their eyes. Everyone listens, and when I finish, applause breaks out. Then we move on to other surveys. Yasmin and I smile all the way — until it's time for Anil's group.

While the other two kids in his group seem happy to talk about their solar power survey, Anil looks sad, sad, sad.

Okay, that is an opinion. My opinion.

Fact: Anil does not smile. Out of the corner of my eye, I can see that Yasmin has noticed that, too.

16

If I Don't ...

THAT EVENING, WE step onto the roof through the narrow doorway at the top of the stairs. We are at the very top of Serene Towers, Block III. "There it is," Anil says. "See? Told you. It's building a nest."

Spotting us, the bird flap-flap-flaps panicked wings, cheeping and whirring and beak-clacking. Yasmin stifles a gasp.

"I think she's a female," I say. "See? Her feathers aren't that fancy. But I can't tell what kind of bird she is."

She is pale yellow and drab gray. When she sees us standing very still, she goes back to work. She keeps an eye on us as she flies back and forth, bringing twigs and bits of leaves to build that growing nest. Is that spiderweb silk she's carrying in her beak? It is! She's a tiny bird. Beak and all, she's probably no bigger than my hand. What is she? And where's the male? Isn't he going to help her? If she

would slow down, I could see the shape of her beak. But she is a whirlwind with feathers.

She is a builder. Look at that nest! It dangles from the bend of the pipe that runs electrical wires into the building. It is a bag of a nest, hanging like a purse from the loop of its handle.

We stand there for a long time, looking at all the things the little bird is busy adding to her nest — grass, leaves, scraps of plastic, hair, coconut husk, feathers, string, even a piece of cloth.

She has decided we are harmless. She can ignore us and focus on her job.

"Maybe she's a sunbird," I whisper.

"No iridescence?" Yasmin asks.

"That's what I'm thinking. Maybe because she's female? Like peacocks have the fancy feathers and peahens are plain."

Anil stays quiet. He's still worrying, I can tell. Still, for this little rooftop bird,

Birds on the Brain

the questions and problems of people are like passing clouds.

Then a thought flies into my mind and settles down with a sharp little cheep: This is this bird's building project. She doesn't know that the top of this apartment block is going to be pulled to pieces and rebuilt. All she knows is her little nest. Look how hard she has to flap her wings to fly back and forth to build it. She does it for the eggs she'll lay, for the chicks she'll hatch. This is their home.

Mummy says I think too much. Maybe she has a point. Some thoughts make my head hurt. This one turns me inside out and upside down. Who will help this hardworking little bird?

The question tumbles in my mind as we go back downstairs. We stay goodbye to Anil. We walk back home. The street is half blocked for drain repair, so we have to walk in the road and keep a sharp lookout for the traffic zipping past. Drivers beep at us to get out of their way.

We skirt the puddles left by the drain-digging. A bus bumps along behind us. We try to step away, but it comes too fast. We jump over the puddles and scramble to a dry spot.

And right there, leaping to avoid a mud splash, I jump into the answer. I will help the bird. I, Reeni Thomas, will not, cannot, must not stand by. Because if I don't do something, who's going to?

17

The Point of the Story

I HAVE TO race through my homework because going to see that bird on Anil's rooftop took time. The science chapter is all about mosquitoes and how they spread malaria and dengue and chikungunya, which I know is a horrible disease. Anil's grandmother caught it three years ago. Her joints hurt so badly she cried. Anil was quite worried because his Viji Paatti is not someone who cries for nothing.

I am pleased to read that many species of birds eat mosquitoes — barn swallows, cattle egrets, nightjars, drongos. It is good to find out that homework is not a total waste of time.

Before I get Mummy to test me on my spelling words, I ask if she has any more news about the city and the bird count. Are they going to be difficult? Are they going to deny permits to bird-watchers for going on government property and the university, and other places like that with trees and birds?

My mother grumbles. "Nothing. Our city-beat reporter tried to get a statement from the mayor, but he won't even talk about the bird count. Like an ostrich, burying his head in the sand. Refusing to face facts."

"Mummy, ostriches don't really do that," I inform her.

"Is that so?" she says. "I must say you're becoming quite a bird expert, Reeni-ma."

My spelling expertise is less impressive. I stumble through the word list. Mummy calls each word out. She smacks her lips in disapproval whenever I get one wrong.

"Adequate: *qua*, not *qui*." Nobody is quitting here.

"Criticism: *ism,* not *izm*." How can anyone tell from the way it sounds?

Council or *counsel*? Both are correct but have different meanings. I get them both, yay!

I escape at last, so I can finally finish reading *Salim Mamoo and Me*. I read-read-read through young Zai's worries about being different and how she tries to cover up that she can't tell birds apart, even pretends she can't see! That is a lot of covering up. I read all the way to the end, and now I get it, I get it. I get why this is a perfect book for me.

The girl in the story, Salim Ali's niece, starts to recognize birds only when she stops worrying about not being a bird expert like everyone else in her family.

Yasmin always says the point of reading a story at all is to find out what it means. It's not about what happens in the end. It's about why it matters. Here is the point of this story. Quit worrying and you will see what has been right there in front of you all along.

And just like that, the two words that sound the same, *council* and *counsel*, come together in my mind.

Just like that, I know what to do — about one of our problems, at least.

18

Tell-Your-City

AT SCHOOL, SITTING under the mango tree while the teachers walk around keeping an eye on us all, we trade our lunches, half for half. That means Yasmin gives me half of Nadira Aunty's delicious puttu, filled to bursting with grated coconut and soft, soft broken rice. I give her half of my tomato and cheese sandwich.

Between mouthfuls — why does someone else's lunch always taste more delicious than your own? — Yasmin says, "Listen. This is important. I borrowed a handbook of birds from Book Uncle and guess what?

I found our nesting bird."

"You did?"

"I did. And you were right. It's a female sunbird."

Oh, that makes me happy and worried at the same time! Happy because it's always nice to identify a bird. Worried because despite being of least concern (LC), that bird is most certainly in danger. If there was a category of MC (for most concern), I'd give it to that sunbird this minute.

"Have you told Anil?" I ask.

"Not yet," she says.

I look for Anil to tell him right now, but he is busy showing karate dodges to a bunch of kids by the wall. We'll catch him later. At least he's not looking sad and mopey. That is a good thing. What is the point of looking sad and mopey? It doesn't help solve any problems, does it?

I tell Yasmin my plan. "We should counsel the city council. We should tell them why birds matter. We should tell them to let the TV station air the program about the bird count. Facts, Yasmin. Don't you think we should give them facts?"

Yasmin agrees. "Let's tell everyone we know to join us, too." She says there is a new app called Tell-Your-City. The city council is inviting everyone to tell them what they think."

"About anything?" I ask.

"And everything," she says. "Water supply, electricity service, the state of the roads, mobile phone access — you know, stuff like that."

It seems even though we are kids, we have to pay attention to everything because it's all connected to us, even if we are not allowed to vote. In my opinion, that is unfair, but try telling a grown-up that.

Yasmin says, "Wapa was reading about the app in the paper last night."

I am glad that Yasmin's father is a

dedicated newspaper reader. My parents only read their phones, and they never tell me anything, which is why I have to eavesdrop all the time.

"Phone!" I cry. Yasmin looks puzzled. She can't see how my mind has leaped from city councils to phones, so I explain. "I have to get Mummy to lend us her old phone so we can download the bird app."

"Multitask time," she says, as the bell rings and we have to line up to go back in for Tamil and science. "Now we need two apps. Reeni, we can catch two birds —"

"With one phone!" I cry, making everyone turn around to see why we are laughing.

Then she gets serious. "The expression is really 'kill two birds.'"

"Ugh," I say. "Why would anyone want to do that?" We agree that it is a horrible expression. How can some words make you happy, but others make your stomach hurt?

19

Fortunately ... Unfortunately

THE FOLLOWING DAY, when I am rushing through breakfast, I ask Mummy, "Can you lend us your old mobile phone? Remember you said maybe?" You have to remind parents, because sometimes they promise things and then they forget.

"Oh, right," she says. "Sorry, Reeni. I checked that old phone, but unfortunately, it doesn't work anymore."

Unfortunately. Such a disappointing word. It feels like one more pigeon splat on top of so many others. I struggle with it all through the school day. It sits with me even during brighter moments, like when Mrs. Rao takes us to the computer lab and shows us how to set up our surveys on a website, so we can give people the link if they want to save trees and answer our questions virtually.

Fortunately, a solution pops out of an unexpected corner. That corner is the school bus. As we line up to board, the bus driver begins to click his riders in, one by one.

Click-click-click. What's fortunate about that? He's clicking on his phone, that's what. Right there is my solution. I whisper it to Yasmin on the bottom step.

"What?" she whispers back. "No!" Unspoken question: *What would our parents say?* "Reeni," Yasmin says, "are you sure?" *Click-click*, and we're up on the top step.

Am I sure? Dare I ask the bus driver for a favor?

I'm not sure, not at all. But I dare. "Do

you think we can borrow your phone from Friday to Monday?" I ask as politely as I can.

Behind me, Yasmin half gasps, half giggles.

"Can you *borrow* it?" the driver cries, so loudly that for a minute, I think I have offended him.

"If you don't mind," I add quickly.

"*Can* you borrow it?" he yells. "Can *you* borrow it? Can you borrow *it*?"

But then he sees that everyone is staring at him, and he lowers his voice and goes back to being a responsible bus driver. "I would be so happy to give it to you," he says. "You know what would make me even happier? If you birdlings could find a way to throw this phone into the ocean for me, then I would never have to see the wretched thing ever again."

Yasmin looks sideways at me. I look back sideways at her. We can't do that! We can't go around throwing phones into the sea. There are a lot of things we can do, but that's not one of them, is it?

We both look at Anil. He makes an unmistakable na-na-na-na-never karate block.

I try to find the right words. "We can't do that for you, but —" Here I stop to let him know an offer is on the way. "But — if you can *lend* us your phone, we would love to borrow it."

"Lend?" he says, as if he sees a window of hope opening up.

"Yes, from Friday to Monday."

"Really?" he says.

"Guaranteed," I reply. "And then we'll borrow it back at the end of next week. Will that work for you?" I'm thinking fast. We'll be able to set it up and get it back in time for the actual bird count day.

He's not completely delighted when he sees we are not going to get rid of it for

Birds on the Brain

him. Still, grudgingly, he agrees.

It feels like a long, long ride. Anil says he's getting off at our stop today, because once again, it is book return and exchange time.

"Did you talk to your parents yet," I ask, "about the bird?"

He nods. "I told them. But my father is busy. Business travel."

"Anil," I say. "You have to make them focus on this. You want me to —?"

Yasmin gives me a warning headshake, so I stop. Anil looks up at the fan over the bus driver's seat as if he expects inspiration from it.

"Nah," he says. "I'll figure it out."

The bus slow-creaks and pulls up to the St. Mary's Road bus stop. We get off.

20

Time Is Rushing

RETURNS AND EXCHANGES completed, Book Uncle asks us about the istri lady. Is she all right? Have we talked with her recently? He is concerned about her.

"She can't afford to buy an electric iron, you see," he says. "It makes me think about the time when the city told me that I had to get a permit and I knew I couldn't afford it."

We nod. We do remember. It took all our efforts to get the city to stop bullying Book Uncle. When you see something unfair like that, you have to speak up.

"I thought I would have to close down my lending library. You children were such a help to me then, and so was our Ponni. I would like very much to do something in return."

"Should we collect money," I ask, "to buy her an iron?"

He shakes his head. "She's very proud," he says. "She doesn't like taking gifts from people." He has heard there is a state grant opening up soon to help vendors like the istri lady make the transition from coal. Maybe she can apply for that. He says he will help her.

It's a start. But what about the power connection?

"One step at a time," he says.

We tell him we are ready to carry out our survey.

"You know you can count me in, don't you?" he says. Then he hands us each a book and waves us on our way.

Yasmin's book is about a frog who wants to sing. I get one about a girl who has grown a peacock's tail. They have nothing to do with anything, but they look like fun. We could use a little fun.

Anil opens his book to a random page. He chews his lip. He pulls his ear. He looks up at the sky.

"What?" we demand.

"I don't know," he says. He closes the book.

"What's it about?" I ask.

"Small solar projects." He stuffs the book into his bag.

"Solar panels for rooftops?" Yasmin asks.

"No. I mean, I don't know!" Anil cries. He wheels around and executes a swirling goodbye kick at us. Then he runs off, yelling, "Have to go work on my survey." In minutes, he has pushed through the crowd of people around the tea and snacks stall. He's vanished.

Birds on the Brain

"Let him think," Yasmin says. "You know how Anil is. You can't rush him."

I know, I know. Anil doesn't like to be rushed. And any other time, I wouldn't want to rush him. Only now, time is rushing along very, very quickly. That makes me nervous. Being nervous makes me feel as if I am spinning around. That is a slightly nauseating feeling.

"I don't know if any of us can think as fast as we need to right now," I say.

"Come on," Yasmin says. "One step at a time, remember. We have to do our survey."

21

What Has Changed?

WITH THE PROMISE of a phone gleaming in my mind, I hope with all my heart that Anil thinks super fast on his way home. I hope he can talk to his parents super fast, as well, to make them pause the solar installation. As for me, I can't do a thing to help that bird on my own, can I? What was the point of my grand promise to myself? *I will not, cannot, must not stand by.* Now I, Reeni Thomas, am turning into a champion bystander.

The istri lady turns my bystanding into listening. It turns out that she knows all about sunbirds — what a surprise! She tells us that they are called "thain-chittu," or honey-birds, in Tamil, on account of the nectar they sip from flowers, sip-sip-sipping with their long, curvy beaks.

"When I lived in my village," she says, "before I came here, I used to see crowds of them fly in to feed on insects. Oh, how I miss those fields, those gardens!"

She says sunbirds bring good luck. "Finding a nest on your property?" She throws her hands up to the sky in wonder. "Or close by? That is even more good luck." She showers us with assurances. "There will be eggs, of course there will. One or two, most likely. They will hatch. The male will come back — he'll help her feed the babies."

She is as excited as we are. We don't have the heart to tell her about the solar panels.

Instead, we tell her about our survey, which we will carry out this evening. "I will take your survey," she says. Ever since Book Uncle taught her how to read and write and count, she tries to practice those skills every chance she gets.

"Wonderful," Yasmin says.

The istri lady shouts, "Selvaraj!" and her son comes running. "He'll take your survey, too," she says. She orders him to tell the autorickshaw drivers on the corner about it so they can also take it. "Those little birds are important," she says.

Selvaraj nods his head fast-fast, which means he doesn't dare disagree. Right away, he takes off to tell his friends at the auto stand about the survey.

I don't point out that taking the survey is no guarantee that the little nesting birds will be safe. That is because I am in awe. My whole life I have seen her ironing clothes for people up and down St. Mary's Road, and I never once suspected that the istri lady was a secret birder.

Birds on the Brain

As she talks, I see something else. I see that the istri lady is looking different. What has changed? I stare at her, and then I realize what's happened.

She used to chew tobacco all the time. She would spit out the juice in red streams, so you had to jump out of her way when you saw her swishing it, ready to squirt. My parents said that stuff could kill you, and why on earth did she keep on chewing it? Now I see that her jaws are not chew-chew-chewing as usual. I see that her mouth is empty.

"What are you staring at?" she demands.

"Er — nothing," I say, but my hand flies up to my own mouth before I can stop it, so of course, she catches on. She laughs out loud so I am embarrassed and don't know where to look.

"I had terrible pain in my mouth," she explains. "It was teeth. My own teeth were paining me so badly, I can't even tell you. I never felt pain like that before! Oh, how they hurt! Your mother — she's a saint — she took me to a dental clinic. Can you believe that?"

I certainly can. I know firsthand how enthusiastic Mummy is about dragging people to doctors and dentists.

"I wouldn't go at first because I can't afford that kind of thing, but she insisted. Then when we got there — best of all! — we found out it was free! Imagine."

Yasmin and I make appreciative murmurs to show that we are imagining and are also impressed.

"*Takku-takku!*" The istri lady waves both hands, making hammering gestures at her face. "They took out all those teeth and guess what? No more pain."

She says the dentist scolded her for chewing that awful stuff. At first, she wasn't going to listen. But then he said to her, "Maybe you're just not strong enough to give it up." That was when the istri lady really took offense.

"Nobody tells me I am weak," she says. "Never. See, see? Eeee!" She shows us. She's missing a few teeth, but the ones left are now shiny clean. Only a few red streaks are left from years of poison juice.

But when we ask her about her iron, the istri lady deflates like a balloon when you let the air out. No free clinics to solve that problem, she says. "Ey, thain-chittu," she calls up to the sky, "why don't you fly down and bring me a little more luck?"

I don't see luck floating down out of the sky. No flying sunbirds. Not even a pigeon looking for a person's head to bless. I am beginning to suspect that's not how luck works. You have to do something to invite it. We have to help the istri lady. But how? We are clueless.

22

Talking About Birds

WE ARE ARMED with a stack of survey forms and pencils. We have written out our online survey link on little cards. We plan to hand them out to people who want to do this virtually. Have we thought of everything or what?

Respondents. That is what you call a person who takes a survey. Our parents are not respondents this time. We have to explain to them that they shouldn't take it personally. They were in our pilot, so they already know the questions. Explaining uses up valuable time, but what can we do?

Birds on the Brain

Finally, we march out — Yasmin and Reeni, chief surveyors of St. Mary's Road.

"We have to seize the moment," Yasmin says.

"Seize?" I say, "How is it possible to seize a moment?"

"It means we have to use every chance we get," she explains. "Come on, let's get to work."

So that is what we do. We administer our survey to a grand total of fifty-six people. We make sure we tell each of them about Bird Count India. That's easy to do — we show them the sign at the bus stop. It turns out that there are bird count signs at three more bus stops along the road, so we can point everyone to a bus stop sign. We also point them to Book Uncle's lending library, with its fine stock of books about birds and birding.

One of the new signs has a map of the best bird-watching places in the city.

"There." I point to a star that marks a big green patch right in the heart of the city. "That's where the bird count kicks off next week." When we get the phone from the driver tomorrow, we can scan that code and find out everything we need to know.

"Is that Aala Maram Park?" Yasmin asks.

It is — the greenest space in the city with a four-hundred-year-old banyan tree. A place for birders.

"We can't go for the kickoff," Yasmin says. "It's a school day."

She's right. That is unfortunate.

"Still," I suggest, "we can look for birds all day wherever we are. In school, even."

"We can count a lot in the evening," Yasmin adds.

So we keep spreading the word. We tell-tell-tell each of our respondents. "Tell your family. Tell your friends. Tell everyone you know. Bird Count India starts on Friday at

Birds on the Brain

Aala Maram Park. Go there for the opening or join in from wherever you are. Get a bird book. Look for birds, try to identify the ones you see, enter the numbers in the app. Ten minutes? All day? It's your choice."

Book Uncle is a respondent. So is the istri lady. Also Selvaraj and all his autorickshaw-driver friends. And the not-so-newly-married couple in 1B, with the baby on the way.

We knock at the door of 2B, but no one opens. In 2A we find the lady who makes the world's best lime pickle. In 2C, a boy we know and also his grandmother who is retired from the income tax department. We survey them all.

We get to many, many people at the bus stop. We get several more at the tea stall while they are waiting for their steaming cups of tea and plates of crisp potato or plantain chips. A girl at the tea stall offers to share her chips with us.

Birds on the Brain

We decline. That is hard to do. Those fried and salted plantain chips smell delicious. But a surveyor must remain objective, and we worry that eating someone's snacks will interfere with our objectivity.

We survey the tea stall owner.

We survey the fruit man across the road and his wife. We survey many of the fancy people coming out of the very fancy Palm Tree Hotel, and the parking lot attendant at the Palm Tree Hotel.

By the end of the evening, we are exhausted. We have handed out all our cards. Completed surveys float back into our hands like feathers on a breezy day. Tomorrow in school, we will have to compile the numbers. What will they tell us? I can't wait to find out.

Most exciting of all, we can hear people talking all around us. It is fun to hear what they are saying. Up and down St. Mary's Road, people are talking about birds.

23

What? How? Who?

JUST AS I AM getting ready to call it a day — feels more like a couple of days — Mummy calls, "Reeni! Come watch the news."

My parents like us to watch the nightly news together. My father says it is a good thing for young people to be informed about current events, and Mummy is always happy to point out snippets of her editing. A headline here, a footer there, a programming choice somewhere else.

I prepare for the usual tedious minutes of politicians speechifying and commentators commenting.

Then comes this local announcement: "The city parks department has issued a public notice that Aala Maram Park is to be closed from Friday, February eighteenth to Monday, February twenty-first."

"What?" I cry.

"Shh," my parents chorus.

Friday to Monday? It can't be! Those are the exact dates of the bird count.

"All previously scheduled events," says the announcer, "are hereby canceled. Traffic will be rerouted ..." She then proceeds to tangle us in a string of road closings and detours.

Closed? Canceled? What kind of announcement is that? How can the bird count happen in the city if the greenest space of all, the place specially mentioned on the poster, is closed to birders and counters?

"Why?" I wail. "Mummy, do you know?"

She shakes her head.

"Can you find out?" I don't mean to shout, but I can't help myself. This puts the whole bird count on the CR list, which, in birder talk, means critically endangered.

"Shh, Reeni-ma, calm down," Mummy hushes.

"I know you're upset, sweetoo," says Daddy, the peacemaker. "But what can we do? What is the point of getting worked up about things we have no control over?"

He thinks he is being helpful but that is not the case.

Now the news is moving on to heat waves in the north of India and a killer cyclone in Madagascar, and they have left our birds behind.

I say good night to my parents, feeling VU (vulnerable) and DD (data deficient) at the same time. As I drag myself out of the room, I can hear them talking.

Out of habit, I stop to listen.

"She's really fired up about those birds,

isn't she?" Daddy says.

Mummy sighs. "Yes, but I'm worried. This is all politics, and the goondas are in power. They always get their way."

Goondas in power? Why do grown-ups use their precious votes to elect rogues and scoundrels? And why should they always get their way?

I'm not going to let that happen. Not this time. I don't care what it takes. I may not have answers to all the *what, how* and *who* questions hammering at me, but I do have a focus. And yes, I am fed up and fired up.

24

Apples and Oranges

THE NEXT DAY whizzes by in such a storm of data that it turns me dizzy. Mrs. Rao takes us to the computer lab to enter our survey results into the website she has set up just for that purpose. The results get neatly compiled into graphs or tables or pie charts, which pleases Mrs. Rao greatly.

Wait. The data storm settles into patterns I can see. How can so many people (thirty-three out of fifty-six) not know anything about birds? How can eighteen people say they don't like birds? And thirty only maybe want to know more? I mean, what is there to not like about birds? What have they ever done to all you people?

Mrs. Rao says, "Reeni, you can either think about this as a half-empty cup or a half-full one. That is your choice." Oops! Have I been muttering my thoughts instead of thinking them silently? Mrs. Rao, it's clear, is in favor of the half-full approach.

"Wait," I say. "What about all the people I gave the link to? Where are their surveys? If we get more responses, couldn't that change the results?"

She says that's correct, but the school computer tech has to check all those inputs before approving them, because this is a school site. It is a security measure, so those won't be ready until Monday.

"Oh, no!" I cry.

"Reeni," she says. "Patience."

"That sounds like a half-empty cup," I say. "Mrs. Rao, this is really important ... the city ... the park ... Bird Count

India ..." My words dry up, and Mrs. Rao looks puzzled.

Wait a cheeping minute. I see what the problem is. If our survey is apples, and the bird count is oranges, and I want to squeeze them together, what I need is not a cup. It's a phone! And we have one — well, almost.

The bus driver is only too happy to give us his phone right away today. "Why wait until tomorrow?" he sings. He says he will keep track of his riders with a notebook and a pencil, the old-fashioned way, for a day or two. Yasmin is still giving me doubtful looks, but I pay no attention.

"Why don't you like your phone?" I ask.

He says it pings when he's asleep and sends him messages he never asked for. "When you are gone, I will be so happy!" he sings to anyone who will listen. But really, he is singing to his free phone that he never asked for.

Lucky for us, Lina Aunty does not have a suspicious mind like our parents. She never once asks, "Where did you get that phone?"

That afternoon, I arrange to meet her at the La-la-la Restaurant for coffee (Lina Aunty) and pomegranate ice cream (me).

She helps me to download the bird count app and the Tell-Your-City app. She makes an account for us in each one. She shows me how to upload data — bird species and numbers in one app, text messages to the city in the other. Now I am armed with tech skills. I just wish I had more time to mobilize my connections.

25

Surprise, Surprise

WHO SHOULD DROP in at the La-la-la Restaurant right in the middle of my last spoonful of melty-delicious pomegranate ice cream but Anil? He has someone with him — his grandmother. Anil's Viji Paatti is a retired architect who also used to teach at the university. Now she lives in an ancient village house three hours away by train. Every few months, she leaves her beautiful village and her garden full of coconut and mango trees to visit family and friends who insist on living in the crowded city.

"We've been looking for you everywhere, Reeni," Anil says. "I think there's an egg. In the nest. She's sitting in it, and the male is there, too. He brings her insects to eat."

My heart leaps up. The istri lady was right! Now more than ever, we have to keep these birds safe. I seize this moment. "Did you talk to your father?"

"Yes, and he's promised to talk to the building association the minute he gets some free time. I hope he remembers. The work is still supposed to start next week."

Next week? The eggs will not hatch that fast. What is Anil going to do? He looks hopeful, but I don't see any sunbird luck shining right now. Mummy is always telling me that I am too impatient, that I want everything to happen the minute I think of it. Now, I want more time. I want time to be on our side. On the sunbird's side.

Anil's paatti gives me a hug so big I think I am going to get lost in it. "I can't believe how you've grown. You kids have been friends since you were so little." She puts her hands together to show an impossibly tiny size. Her purse falls off her shoulder and Anil picks it up for her.

While Lina Aunty and Viji Paatti chat, the server arrives to welcome the new customers. "Ice cream samples, ma'am, young sir? Mango? Sapota? Surprise flavor of the day?"

Na-na-na-na-no! I want to cry. We don't have time for surprise ice cream. But I work on staying calm while Anil and his grandmother taste their tiny sample scoops and try to guess the flavor.

When the trying and guessing is all done, Viji Paatti tells us the reason for this visit. One of her former students recently won a prize for best green design, so she has been invited to attend a Smart City meeting. It is the first in a series of meetings that the city is planning to hold.

"I'm very proud of her," she says.

"That's wonderful," Lina Aunty says. "I should tell my manager at the bank. I bet she'd like to attend that meeting." Then she says goodbye, whispers, "Good luck, Reeni" in my ear and takes off.

"What's a smart city?" I ask.

Viji Paatti's explanation is filled with GPS-enabled bikes, mapping systems, solar energy — panels, chargers, grid connections — digital signs, data centers, apps for parking and disaster response and lots more. Some of it wafts right over my head, but it all sounds important and shiny new.

One thing catches my attention. "Did you say green spaces?"

"Yes, yes," says Anil's grandmother. "Public spaces like gardens and parks. They reduce pollution, give people places to walk and exercise ..." Green spaces are her student's special interest, so she ends up telling us how important it is to work very hard to do what you love.

She says it is a global movement. Cities all over the world are trying to use smart technology.

Global? And local, too, right? Very, very local? Why not?

"Anil," I say. "Your book was about small solar projects, right?"

"Right."

"Anil is getting to be quite an engineer," Viji Paatti says encouragingly.

"And your solar tech group can work on things like that."

"Yeah — so?"

I want to leap up from my seat and dance around the La-la-la Restaurant. I want to spread surprise and delight and my iridescent new idea.

"Anil," I say. "Could one of those solar tech people build a solar-power charger for you? Or help you to build one? For an electric iron? Can you ask them?"

His mouth falls open. "Reeni!" he says slowly, "Yes. I could. I will. We're all meeting tomorrow. They're going to help us do the solar survey. Hey, Reeni, I never even thought of that!" Then he leaps up from his seat. He runs around our table and executes a lightning-fast series of kicks and punches into the air. He shouts a triumphant "Hiya!"

Of course he'll ask. Of course he will. It's so simple. A win-win-win. When you help someone, they want to help you back.

26

Tell ... Tell ... Tell ...

WHEN I GET HOME, Mummy is reading a text message on her phone. "From your teacher," she says.

She skims the text. "Your bird count is going to be a special activity for your class next week." She scrolls down, down, down. That is one long message. "I don't know if I need to reply or anything. Do I have to give permission?"

"What?" I say, alarmed. "Of course you have to give permission. Say yes. You wouldn't think of saying no, would you?"

She laughs. "I'm not a total spoilsport,"

she says, and she texts back YES.

What a relief! There I was thinking that once again I was at the mercy of parents who are sometimes, let's face it, DD (data deficient).

Mummy reads me part of the text. It says we will be out of the classroom, in and around the school grounds, counting birds. But, I think, we will not be walking to Aala Maram Park. It is close to our school. We could walk there easily. Only, of course, it will be closed.

Mummy says in the afternoon we will go back inside. We will tally all the birds we counted and enter our counts into the database.

That reminds me. "Why is the park closed? Did you find out?"

She sighs. "Party meeting," she says and shakes her head as if she is shaking the mayor and his party out of her thoughts.

We still need more tell-tell-tell. We all

need to Tell-Your-City.

So that is what we do. The rest of the afternoon, we tell everyone we know and lots of people we don't know as well. Every spare minute until it starts to get dark, Yasmin and I go up and down St. Mary's Road, again and again.

"Tell the city to let the bird count go ahead."

"Tell the city to open up Aala Maram Park for the bird count."

"Join the bird count."

"Tell the city. Look! Here's the app."

"Download the app. We can show you how."

"Let us tell you why birds matter. Did you know …?"

"Let us tell you …"

"Tell … tell … tell …"

By the time the parrots have settled down in the feathery-leafed branches of the raintree, we have done so much telling

Birds on the Brain

that our throats are sore. We drag ourselves back home to Horizon Apartment Flats. We are exhausted and blistered. Yasmin's blister is on her left little toe. Mine is on my right big toe. We share blisters and we also share big smiles.

We have collected our data and thought about how we can use it. We have sorted out facts from opinions — well, mostly. We have done good work. And maybe, just maybe, all those messages will get through to the mayor and the big-big politicians at city hall, and they will open up the park and let the bird count go forward as it should.

We all need birds, whether we know it or not. They work hard for us all the time. They eat insects and grubs. They spread seeds, which grow into plants that cool the air and help stop soil erosion. The planet needs birds, and don't we all live on the very same planet? It's DD to be putting birders in cages by telling them that they can't enter the greenest park in the city for such an important local and global event.

27

No Reason to Cheer

TALKING OVER AND around the nightly news, I tell my parents about my good idea — a solar charger for the electric iron that the istri lady will buy with the grant that Book Uncle helps her write. They are delighted.

The surprise ice cream flavor at the La-la-la Restaurant was coconut milk. From now on, whenever I taste coconut milk ice cream, I will think of the sunshiny power of a good idea.

"You see?" Daddy says. "As I always say, for every problem, there is a possible solution that is good for everyone. The trick is to have a clever friend like your Anil who can carry it out."

"Our Reeni is also clever," Mummy points out, "to come up with the idea."

They agree on my cleverness. That is nice. Mummy seems to have completely forgotten my daydreaminess and habit of wasting time on the roof.

But not all surprises are pleasant. My mother says that since the city invited feedback from the public, the TV station invited the mayor to a live call-and-text chat. They want him to answer questions from the audience and from callers, as well as via the Tell-Your-City app.

Yay! We can use the app to send in our opinions and questions!

I almost say that. Then I remember, just in time, that my parents do not know about the phone we have borrowed from the bus driver. They don't know about the apps that Lina Aunty has helped us to download. So I bite back my words. All I let myself say is the yay part.

But there is no reason to cheer. "The mayor's office turned us down," Mummy says.

"What?"

She shakes her head. "Sorry, Reeni. They said they're too busy getting ready for the Smart City meetings at the mayor's office." She says the city is working on using technology to change how people live.

"Oh, that meeting on Saturday?" I say.

"You know about it?" Daddy looks at me over the rim of his glasses.

I tell them about Anil's grandma and her student. "And doesn't smart also mean green?" I ask. "Not just high tech, right? Is the government really smart if it doesn't help birders and birds?"

My parents look surprised at all this.

"They can't ignore us!" I cry, feeling every word. "We can't let them! We have to —" That stops me short. I was about to say, *We have to bombard them with the Tell-Your-City app.* But wait a squawking minute! I can't tell my parents that.

Oh, that phone! I was so sure that borrowing it was a great idea. Maybe, after all, it wasn't.

It feels funny — not laughing funny but weird, I mean — to be hiding that phone from my parents. Yes, it's nice when they think I am clever. But this hiding side of me? I don't like it. It makes me feel flattened, dull. Not even a little bit iridescent.

The secret of the phone grows heavier the more I think about it. It weighs me down.

28

Frantic Mind

THAT NIGHT, I BRUSH my teeth and tell myself to calm down. *Calm down, Reeni!* I say it silently over and over again. On Monday, we can return the bus driver's phone and then we don't have to worry about it — for one more week.

And after that — just one more quick borrow. What's the problem? But there is a part of me that fights back. It's not a thing you're supposed to do, borrow phones from people if you don't have permission from home or school. Especially when the phone was given to that someone by the school and it wasn't meant for random things like bird counts and arguing with city hall.

No problem at all, Calm Reeni says. *We'll only borrow it back one time, only for the bird count. Which is important, isn't it?* Panicky Reeni has to agree.

With every brush stroke, I foam up more toothpaste. With every brush stroke, Calm Reeni wins a bit more courage.

Then the phone starts pinging. It pings and pings and pings. Every single ping sounds louder than the last. Every single one hits me right between the eyes.

I have to get to that phone! I have to shut it off before my parents hear it! How can they not hear it already? That pinging is so loud I bet half of St. Mary's Road can hear it.

Pthpffthh! I'm trapped in a cloud of toothpaste. All over my mouth. All over my hands. I try to seize the moment — and the phone.

Birds on the Brain

But. It's. Too. Late.

There is Mummy in the bathroom doorway with the bus driver's phone in her hand. "What is this, Reeni? Where did you get this phone and what exactly is going on?" she asks.

That is how the whole unhappy explanation chokes its way out of panicky me, even if it's slightly muffled by cinnamon-and-ginger-flavored toothpaste.

The result of my confession? Unhappiness all around.

I'm unhappy for all kinds of reasons that are fighting for room in my mind. My troublesome secret has been found out. I don't like being in trouble. I also don't like what I did. I feel small and mean.

Mummy is unhappy because I lied, or didn't tell the truth, which, she says, is the same thing. She drives this point home several times to make sure I get it. Daddy has joined the parental force, which is what usually happens when I'm in trouble.

My parents are most unhappy that I have taken —

"Borrowed," I say. "We have borrowed …" That does not help.

"Taken an official phone," Daddy says,

Birds on the Brain

"from a school employee — what was *he* thinking, anyway, to hand it over to you just like that?"

"Never mind him," says Mummy. "I want to know, what was Reeni thinking?"

I mumble that the driver hates his phone.

"That is his problem," says my mother, "not yours. And now will you kindly tell us what was all that beeping about?"

"Let me see," Daddy says. Mummy hands him the phone. He *click-click-clicks* his way into the app to take a look. "What's this? Tell-Your-City? This is a reply to your message, blah blah …"

"Your message?" Mummy demands. "Who are you writing to?"

"Oh, Reeni," says Daddy. "You sent messages to the city council? To the mayor? For what?" Am I imagining it or is that a smile doing its best to hide behind the exasperated look on my father's face?

"Better tell us everything right now," Mummy says. She is not hiding any smiles.

I try to say any one of a dozen things that pop at once into my frantic mind. Not one of them follows the normal pathway from my brain and out of my mouth. Instead, a big lump comes into my throat from I don't know where. My eyes fill up, no matter how hard I try to blink them dry. I burst into tears.

29

The Olympic Sport of Mind-Changing

THE NEXT MORNING, we declare a truce, my parents and I. Explanations are involved, and an apology. Mine.

My parents concede that it is unfair that children do not usually get asked their opinions. "Life is not always fair," Mummy says. She gives me the kind of taken-aback look that parents get when they think they know you but then they see that you have grown.

They do insist on one thing. I have to return that phone. Today. Right away.

I tell Yasmin everything on the walk to the bus stop. She listens. She makes sympathetic noises. She does not say I told you so.

We give the phone back to the driver. He opens his mouth as if he wants to say something, but then he closes it again.

On our way to school, as we chat in low voices to match our mood, I keep an eye on the driver. As he turns under the flyover where a famous old movie studio used to be and there is now a shiny-bright hotel, I see his shoulders droop. We stop. The lights change. We go around the circle. Usually, at this point, he tells a joke or bursts into song. Not today.

I really want to tell our bus driver that I'm sorry we were not able to lose the phone on his behalf. Normally, my words would come bursting out. Now I think, you can't make everyone happy all the time. Sometimes it is better not to say anything.

We arrive in school. While we're getting

off the bus — we're the last ones off — I am silent, but Yasmin speaks up. She says, "Mobile phones can be useful, you know, driver sir. They're not all bad." She tells him about the bird count app that Lina Aunty loaded for us onto his phone.

"Show me," he says, practically throwing the phone back at us.

We show him. We also show him how he can turn off the phone at night so it doesn't keep waking him up. He looks encouraged.

"You can use the phone only when you want to," Yasmin says.

"You can count birds," I add, "not just students riding your bus."

"Ah, hmm," he says. "And what will they do with the numbers of birds that I tell them I have counted?"

We tell him how our numbers from right here in our city will go into a worldwide database so that people who study birds will learn more. We — the "we" who are all people living in the big-big world — will learn more.

"About birds?"

"Yes."

"Worldwide?"

"Yes."

"*Worldwide*, ah? Like the Olympics?"

"Um, kind of like that," I say. Then I tell him about the Tell-Your-City app. His eyes grow wide.

"Oh?" he says. "I can do that? There is a leak in a water pipe on my street. Such a waste."

"Tell them," we say. "That's what the app is for."

He nods his head slowly. He says, "That is good. Yes, good. Who would have thought?" He puts the phone in his shirt pocket and gives it a pat or two.

We get off the bus, leaving him humming a little tune.

30

Clear as Birdsong

MY PARENTS GREET Saturday morning by loading me up with things to do. They believe that an apology in words must be reinforced by actions. But my mistakes have to do with honesty and thinking before you act, so how does cleaning a room make up for that? It's no use arguing, though, so I do it anyway.

Daddy stops by to offer encouragement. He opens the curtains so there's more light for me to see what I'm doing.

Mummy stops in to remind me that I can't stuff all that junk under the bed.

Cleaning up doesn't mean simply hiding the mess.

My second have-to, after the room has been spic-and-spanned to Mummy's satisfaction, is tidying up the entry hall where everyone takes their shoes off before coming in. I put shoes, sandals and flip-floppy chappals back on the shelf, and oh, yes, I have to dust the shelf first.

My third have-to is taking the laundry down from the clothesline and folding it. I try not to show my glee at this task, as it lets me race up to the rooftop.

I yank the clothes off the line as fast as I can. Then I look around, hoping to see what's going on in the trees.

A few crows are chatting back and forth. I count five parrots flying out of the silk cotton tree across the road. A mynah stalks a lizard — a gecko, to be precise — along the edge of the wall.

I'm about to go back down when a flash

of blue catches my eye. On the highest branch of the raintree, practically eye level with me, is a sunbird. Definitely a sunbird, no question. It's a male. His dark spring plumage has come alive in sunlight.

He hops along the branch to its very tippy-tip, and sunshine lights him up in brilliant blue. I can make out maroon and purple streaks.

He opens his curving beak and snaps it. I think maybe he's snatching mosquitoes, but then he starts to sing. His song starts off with a soft, rattly beat. It builds and builds. His beak opens and shuts and opens again. His little tongue darts out, in, out. The song explodes into a trilling *chwee-chwee-chwee* that shakes up his whole body. I have never seen anything like it. He's calling all the girl birds for miles around, looking for a partner.

The bird and his song settle inside me. Through folding the clothes and putting them away, that sweet song echoes in my head. All the time I thought Anil's survey idea linking solar power and karate was small and uninteresting. Now I see how big it is. It is local *and* global — as much as Bird Count India and every bit as important.

It makes me feel all tangled up inside to see that if anyone was small and selfish, it was me.

All kinds of connections explode in my brain. I remember another tangled time, back when we were helping Book Uncle. I thought Yasmin wasn't listening to me, so I couldn't tell her how I felt, which made me not listen to her, and what a terrible loop that was! Can't let that kind of thing happen now.

At last, I'm released from parental detention! I find the phone handset hiding under a kitchen towel. I tap-tap-tap Anil's number.

Birds on the Brain

"Have you done your survey yet?" I ask.

He says his solar power and karate survey went well. Quite a few people signed up to support the fundraiser. Some people even said they'd like to be part of the project. They'd like to get panels installed where they live.

The birdsong in my brain turns into the beautiful dance of data landing in the right column. "Anil," I say. "You have to find those people. Connect them with your solar tech group."

"I did already," he says.

"Then follow up," I say. "Get them talking to each other. Fast."

"Why?" He sounds surprised.

I tell him. If enough people are interested in booking the trainees to put panels in their buildings, then the trainers will have many new sites. They can then easily push Anil's building to the back of the line, can't they?

Crash!

"Anil?" I say, "Are you there?"

Silence. Then, "Sorry, Reeni, I dropped the phone." He says he'll ask. Right away. Of course he will.

I run across the hall to tell Yasmin. She says, "Wonderful. You're right. They can change their plans."

"Exactly," I say, "people can change their minds. Even stubborn people."

She wrinkles her nose. "What are you saying?"

It's clear as birdsong, clear as data, clearer than clear. "Like the bus driver. If his no can become a maybe and maybe even become a yes …"

"Yes …?"

"Yasmin, the first Smart City meeting is today!" I say. "It's open to the public. We should go. We should give the mayor some good reasons to change his mind."

31

Uninvited

I ASK. I ASK AGAIN. I coax. I wheedle. I beg and plead.

Mummy tries to convince me that "open to the public" doesn't mean they really want anyone to go. "It won't be interesting, Reeni," she says. "Quite the opposite. City council meetings are deadly. Trust me. I've been to a few."

When she sees I won't quit, she agrees to drive Yasmin, Anil and me to city hall to attend the Smart City meeting.

Here's who else shows up. Anil's grandmother, of course, to see her student, who is going to be there onstage with all the official people. Lina Aunty and her boss, the bank manager. Book Uncle.

"You told everyone to be here?" Mummy asks me.

I make maybe-I-did noises. She sighs. "Oh, Reeni, Reeni."

Who else? The istri lady. Her son, Selvaraj, with some of his autorickshaw driver friends. Her older son who is visiting from the village, along with his wife and their two children. The not-so-newly-married couple in 1B Horizon Apartment Flats. The lady from 2A who makes the world's best lime pickle. The boy and his grandmother from 2C. The school bus driver. The fruit man and his wife. The tea stall owner. The tea stall owner's sister and brother-in-law. Several regular tea stall customers. Looking around the gathering crowd, I recognize many of the people who took our survey.

Birds on the Brain

We tell the pair of staffers at the door that we are here for the Smart City meeting.

"Do you have invitations?" they ask. Anil's grandmother has one. She has been invited because her student is here. They let her in. The rest of us? We must be uninvited.

Book Uncle clears his throat. "We are the public," he says. "The notice in the newspaper said this meeting is open to the public."

The staffers scurry inside. Then they come back and usher us into a very full room. All the chairs are taken, so we have to stand against the wall.

We wait for the meeting to start. We wait for three minutes. Five. At thirteen minutes, the mayor appears with a little group of city council members. They take their places on the stage. I see Anil's grandmother leaning over a young woman who is showing her something on a laptop. That must be her student.

Fifteen minutes. Nineteen. Twenty-two.

Finally, when I am full to bursting from waiting, the mayor flashes a smile around the room. He welcomes the council members one by one. He welcomes the invited experts. He welcomes the tech consultants. "And" — he casts a puzzled look around the room — "finally, welcome, of course, to members of the public. We did not know there would be so much interest. Please … have a seat …" He waves both hands toward the ceiling as if chairs are going to appear by magic for the invited-uninvited public.

We stay standing. The meeting starts. It goes on. And on. And on. It is all about agendas and budgets and projections. I hear a few words I know — *data, charts,* even *surveys* — but I can't put them together to make any sense. I can't understand what anyone is saying, not even Viji Paatti's student, who shows slides with plans and blueprints and tables with numbers. Viji Paatti probably gets it. But I don't.

Mummy was right. They don't really want us here. *Counsel the council?* What was I thinking? These are important people with agendas and budgets. Why did I ever think they would make time for me and my friends? I am not smart enough for this Smart City meeting.

32

Seizing the Moment

WHILE I AM sinking into being unsmart and uninvited, the conversation on the stage winds down. The mayor announces that it's public question time.

"This is not my meeting," he says. Really? He could have fooled me. "For your information, my most loyal and *engaged* members of the public, this is *your* meeting. Therefore ..." He looks up at the clock, as if that will speed it up. "Any comments or questions?"

Here is my moment. I should seize it. But I can't. Something is not right. The mayor is asking what we think, it's true. But he sounds — *fake*. As if he hopes no actual questions or comments will fly out and hit him on the head.

I try to raise my hand, but it will not go up.

Silence. Then a question. A panelist answers.

"Mumble-babble-blah green spaces blah-blah," someone says.

"Blah-grumble green spaces babble-mumble," someone replies.

It goes on a little longer.

Two words break through to me. In between the words I can't hear and the words I don't understand, there is that signal like a big green flag waving in my face: *green spaces, green spaces, green spaces.*

I feel my hand going up. I hear a slightly wobbly voice. "I have a question."

That is my voice. I've spoken out loud. Everyone turns to look at me. Now what

do I do? For a moment, I wish a hole in the ground would open up. I wish it would swallow me whole, like a bird snapping up a mosquito.

Yasmin grabs my other hand and squeezes it. To my left, Anil delivers a quick air punch. Just like that, I know I am not alone.

My question shakes itself free. "Bird Count India is next week," I say. "So why is Aala Maram Park closed for a party meeting during the bird count?"

The mayor and the councillors talk over each other. "What?" "Where?" "Who?" "Why?" Then the mayor says crossly, "Bird count, bird count? Why is this bird count so important?"

"Because," I say, "it's local and global. Isn't that like your Smart City plan?"

He narrows his eyes at me. "Yes, but last year, it was a big fiasco. They said our numbers went down. How can this be?"

"Too many trees chopped," I answer. "Too much construction and not enough nesting places."

"Who says so? Some foreign group?" He takes the famous Karate Samuel stance that was on all his election campaign posters. "How do I know this is not fake news, hah?"

"Because," I say, "it's your own city residents doing the counting. It's us. If the numbers are down, isn't that data important for your Smart City plan? And if you close up green spaces, then how can we give you any data?"

Others call out.

"Yes, yes!"

"Listen to the child."

"Here's a green space so why not let us use it?"

"Hold your rally somewhere else!"

I recognize some of the voices. The bus driver says, "Aala Maram Park is for the public, not for politicians." Mummy pipes up, "Let the press cover the bird count!"

I look around the little circle of people I know who have all come to support me and my friends. I say, "Istri-amma, tell everyone about the birds in your village."

"Me?" she says. "Now?" I nod.

"Mayor Karate Samuel, sir," I say, in my clearest, politest voice. "Here is someone with a comment."

The mayor looks at his councillors. They look up, down, sideways, at different corners of the room. But they have to listen.

The istri lady takes a breath. Then she begins to recite Tamil bird names. "Mayil, meen kothi, kuyil." Peacocks fan their tails in my mind when she speaks their name. Kingfishers and koels spread their wings. Who knew words could work magic like this? "Theyyal chittu, thavittu kuruvi." I picture tailor birds sewing leaves into nests and yellow-billed babblers in their chattering flocks. Bird names echo from the high roof of the city council chamber.

At the end of this list poem, the istri lady says, "Those are the birds in my village. They sing in the voices of heaven. Who in this city has even heard birds like that?"

The mayor and the councillors are in a trance, as if they are straining to see and hear those birds. The room is so quiet you could have heard a feather drop.

Now I know just what to say. I tell them more about Bird Count India, about our survey. "Birds don't vote," I say, "but they share our city with us. You know what? If we have a truly green city with space for birds — why, that will be good for people, too." I breathe, and the words find their way.

"Birds matter," I continue. "That's why we decided to focus on birds, and books about birds. Many of you here today took

Birds on the Brain

our survey. So what made you decide to show up now? Maybe you're here because you care about birds. Maybe you want to know more about smart cities. Maybe both."

I take my time. I have to make every word count. "Because *no* and *maybe* can change into *yes*. We need that change. The bird count will help us to focus on birds. It will bring our birds into a global database. But how can we make that happen if the park is closed for the count? Those birds the istri lady talked about? The fact is, we *can* hear some of those birds, right here in the city. I've even seen some of them. We just have to make time to watch and listen." I stop here.

"We have to make quiet spaces," says Yasmin.

"Safe spaces." Anil karate-blocks all maybes.

The mayor snaps out of his trance. He

looks at us standing there, with Anil in his karate uniform, blue belt and all. The mayor looks. Slowly, he smiles. He bows to Anil, karate style.

"Children," he says, as if he has never uttered a more marvelous word. "Congratulations. You are the youngest contributors to our innovative Smart City planning process. The park will be open. Count on it." He flashes his famous smile. "Get it, ha ha?! Bird count? Count on it?" The councillors laugh dutifully.

"I myself," the mayor promises, "will report to Aala Maram Park at seven o'clock in the morning for the bird count opening. So will these fine public servants — elected by you, the voting public — distinguished members of your very own city council." The councillors trade squirmy looks. "All will be there," says the mayor firmly.

Viji Paatti's student, architect and planner, invited green spaces expert, starts clapping, slow and sure, *thatta-thatta-thatta*, like a conductor leading a band. The room erupts with cheers and shouts and wild applause.

33

A Flash of Iridescence

"QUIET, QUIET." A week later, that is what we say, over and over, on the morning of the bird count at Aala Maram Park.

It is hard for the city officials to listen rather than talk, but we can see that they are trying. "Speeches are fine," we say, "but keep them quick and quiet."

Mayor Samuel cuts a ribbon to open the day. Our city becomes the first in India to be an official sponsor of Bird Count India, maybe the first to recognize that birds = green = smart.

A group of women have been here since

five this morning, they tell us. They add final pinches of rice flour to their kolam design. It has two peacocks facing each another, a flower between them. Their tails join, spreading over the ground in an elegant fan to welcome us all.

A few at a time, the kids in my class arrive. Mrs. Rao comes with an armload of notepads and pencils and spare binoculars for anyone who needs them. She counts noses. Are we all here? She gives instructions. We'll work in groups. ("Yes, Reeni, friends can work together.") One person in each group will keep count.

Yasmin has brought us birding books for reference. Anil is wearing a big smile. He tells us that the rooftop solar project is now officially delayed. The association has been allowed to postpone the work until the sunbirds are all done with their nest.

Aala Maram Park turns into a birding hotspot. Enough people show up that the

Birds on the Brain

city closes nearby roads to cars and buses and autorickshaws, bikes and motorbikes and scooters and anything with wheels. Permits have been quickly granted to make this possible. Bus routes have been changed for today so that green spaces can also become quiet spaces. Pedestrians are welcome, but no dogs, please. Today, we make room for living things with beaks and wings.

One of the city councillors has invited official representatives from Bird Count India. They show us how to track our sightings in our notebooks to enter later on the national website. They teach cell phone users nifty app tricks. They have brought bird ID posters to help us know what we're spotting.

They take our pictures, just us three. "Our youngest bird count organizers," they say. Cameras whir and click. A crew from the TV station arrives to film the count.

Soon we start to spread out through the green and waiting park. Some people will spend a little time here before they go to work. Others might come later. Others yet might look for birds on their own streets, their own rooftops.

From out of a tangle of banyan tree roots, we're greeted by a long cry, half-cackle, half-mew. A peacock!

Oh, joy! I listen for cheeps and chirps, squawks and screeches. I adjust my binoculars. I squint up into blurry layers of green. I scan the trees for hints of wings, glimpses of feathers and beaks. For a flash of iridescence.

UMA KRISHNASWAMI was born in India and now lives in Victoria, British Columbia. Her other publications include *Two at the Top*, illustrated by Christopher Corr; *Book Uncle and Me*, illustrated by Julianna Swaney, winner of the ILA Social Justice Literature Award; and *The Girl of the Wish Garden*, illustrated by Nasrin Khosravi. She has been nominated twice for the prestigious Astrid Lindgren Memorial Award. Uma is faculty emerita, Writing for Children and Young Adults, Vermont College of Fine Arts.

JULIANNA SWANEY grew up bird-watching with her dad, and birds have always had an important place in her life. She has illustrated numerous books for children and spends her time at her home in Oregon painting, gardening and daydreaming.